WORLD OF WOW WONDER

THE AWESOME BOOK OF

FLESH-EATERS

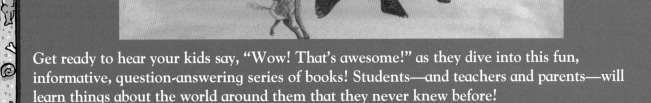

Get ready to hear your kids say, "Wow! That's awesome!" as they dive into this fun, informative, question-answering series of books! Students—and teachers and parents—will learn things about the world around them that they never knew before!

This approach to education seeks to promote an interest in learning by answering questions kids have always wondered about. When books answer questions that kids already want to know the answers to, kids love to read those books, fostering a love for reading and learning, the true keys to lifelong education.

Colorful graphics are labeled and explained to connect with visual learners, while entertaining explanations of each subject will connect with those who prefer reading or listening as their learning style.

This educational series makes learning fun through many levels of interaction. The in-depth information combined with fantastic illustrations promote learning and retention, while question and answer boxes reinforce the subject matter to promote higher order thinking.

Teachers and parents love this series because it engages young people, sparking an interest and desire in learning. It doesn't feel like work to learn about a new subject with books this interactive and interesting.

This set of books will be an addition to your home or classroom library that everyone will enjoy. And, before you know it, you too will be saying, "Wow! That's awesome!"

"People cannot learn by having information pressed into their brains. Knowledge has to be sucked into the brain, not pushed in. First, one must create a state of mind that craves knowledge, interest, and wonder. You can teach only by creating an urge to know." - Victor Weisskopf

© 2014 Flowerpot Press

Contents under license from Aladdin Books Ltd.

Flowerpot Press
142 2nd Avenue North
Franklin, TN 37064

Flowerpot Press is a Division of Kamalu LLC, Franklin, TN, U.S.A. and Flowerpot Children's Press, Inc., Oakville, ON, Canada.

ISBN 978-1-4867-0341-8

Written by:
Michael Benton

Illustrators:
Ross Watton (SGA)
Sarah Smith
Cartoons: Jo Moore

American Edition Editor:
Johannah Gilman Paiva

Designer: Flick, Book Design & Graphics

American Redesign:
Jonas Fearon Bell

Copy Editor:
Kimberly Horg

Educational Consultant:
Jim Heacock

Printed in China.

CONTENTS

INTRODUCTION

Discover for yourself the most amazing things about these ferocious creatures that roamed Earth millions and millions of years ago. What did they eat? How did they live?

Spot and count!

Where did they go? What new discoveries are scientists making? Chapter by chapter, this book gives you the latest information about these fearsome meat eaters, from the smallest turkey-sized dinosaurs to the amazing Tyrannosaurus rex. Learn about how flesh-eating dinosaurs became fossils—where they are found and who looks for them—and find out how you can name a dinosaur after yourself!

Q: Why watch out for these boxes?

A: They give answers to the dinosaur questions you always wanted to ask.

zoom in on...

Dinosaur bits
Look out for these boxes to take a closer look at flesh-eaters' features.

Awesome facts
Watch out for these diamonds to learn more about the truly weird and wonderful facts about flesh-eaters and their world.

WHEN THEY LIVED

Dinosaurs lived between 230 and 65 million years ago (mya). This is a very long time ago. It's hard enough to imagine hundreds of years ago, let alone millions. Dinosaurs are dated according to the geological time scale, which is used to age rocks. Geologists figure out the ages of ancient rocks by studying radioactive elements in them, and by analyzing fossils.

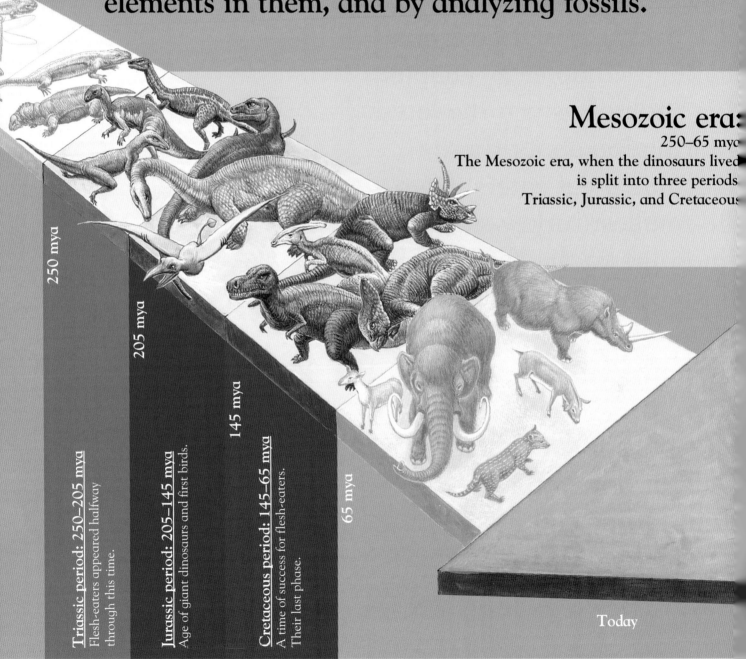

Mesozoic era:
250–65 mya
The Mesozoic era, when the dinosaurs lived, is split into three periods, Triassic, Jurassic, and Cretaceous.

250 mya

205 mya

145 mya

65 mya

Triassic period: 250–205 mya
Flesh-eaters appeared halfway through this time.

Jurassic period: 205–145 mya
Age of giant dinosaurs and first birds.

Cretaceous period: 145–65 mya
A time of success for flesh-eaters. Their last phase.

Today

At the start of the age of the dinosaurs, the continents were all joined together as one great supercontinent called "Pangaea." Over millions of years, the Atlantic Ocean opened up and Pangaea split apart. The continents drifted (moved slowly) to their present positions. They are still moving about an inch (a few centimeters) each year.

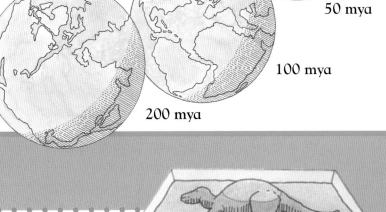

Today

50 mya

100 mya

200 mya

Continental drift

Pangaea —

Q: How did a flesh-eating dinosaur become a fossil?

A: Small meat-eating animals ate the flesh from the dead dinosaur's bones. Some bones rotted. Others were buried under layers of sand or mud. These turned into fossils over time, as tiny spaces in the bones filled with rock. Millions of years later, the fossilized bones are uncovered by water or wind action. Paleontologists dig the fossilized bones out of the rock and clean them, making sure they don't fall apart. They make maps and take photographs at the dig site so that they can tell later exactly where everything was found.

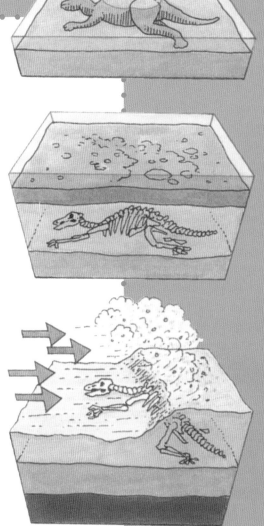

FLESH-EATERS

Flesh-eating dinosaurs, called "theropods," ranged from turkey-sized dinosaurs to the awesome Tyrannosaurus rex. Theropods of different sizes ate prey of different sizes. This meant that several species could live side-by-side.

In the Late Cretaceous of Canada, smaller meat eaters lived alongside the huge T. rex. Troodon hunted lizards, mammals, and even insects. It relied on speed and intelligence. Ornithomimus ate small plant-eating dinosaurs and the young of larger ones.

Big meat eaters, like T. rex, ate the larger plant eaters. T. rex probably wasn't very fast or very bright. It didn't need to be. It was so big, it could attack almost any other dinosaur.

T. rex used its massive teeth to tear strips from prey's flesh.

Troodon

WHAT MAKES A FLESH-EATER?

All flesh-eaters had sharp claws and sharp, curved teeth that pointed backwards. So if the prey struggled, it moved further into the gaping jaws. One of the most fearsome flesh-eaters was Deinonychus.

Deinonychus

Q: How did Deinonychus use its toe claw?

A: It had one huge claw on each foot, on the second toe. When running, it held the claw off the ground so it would not become blunt. But when it attacked, its victim raised its foot and slashed downwards, through a half circle.

Deinonychus was only as tall as a ten-year-old child, so it had to work in packs to bring down large prey like this Tenontosaurus.

Tenontosaurus

zoom in on...

Balancing

Two-legged dinosaurs were like see-saws, balanced over their back legs. The front of the body had to weigh the same as the tail, or the dinosaur would fall on its nose. So flesh-eaters had to hold their backbones nearly flat when they ran, and flick their massive tails around to keep perfect balance.

Awesome facts
Most dinosaurs were not very smart, but Deinonychus had a big brain. It had to have a good sense of balance, excellent eyesight, and be able to communicate.

MAKING A MARK

The first flesh-eating dinosaur was Herrerasaurus from the Late Triassic of Argentina, 230 million years ago. Medium-sized and good at hunting, Herrerasaurus liked to eat mammal-like reptiles called "cynodonts," which lived in burrows.

Herrerasaurus

Herrerasaurus had the advantage in a sudden attack. It could creep up silently, dart its head into a cynodont burrow, and race off with a cub before the parent could do anything.

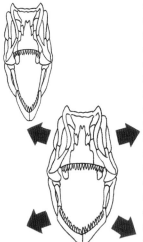

Q: How did dinosaur jaws open so wide?

A: Most theropods had very narrow skulls. There wasn't much in there except teeth and jaw muscles—the brain was pretty tiny. But when a theropod opened its jaws, its whole mouth stretched sideways to make a bigger bite.

The ancestors of mammals belonged to the same mammal-like reptile group as cynodonts. Some cynodonts probably had hair and were warm-blooded. They could hunt at night, unlike the cold-blooded early dinosaurs.

Theropods all had powerful hands. Early ones, like Herrerasaurus, had four or five muscular fingers, each armed with a long, sharp claw. Later, theropods generally had only three fingers, and some, like T. rex, had only two.

Cynodont

Predator numbers

Theropods were rarer than plant-eaters. This is because there must always be far fewer predators than prey animals, similar to lions and antelope today.

HUNT TO THE DEATH

Fossilized footprints show that dinosaurs walked and swam in lakes. Ceratosaurus was the terror of North America 150 mya. But at 20 feet (6 m) long, it took more than one Ceratosaurus to bring down the monster Apatosaurus, 69 feet (21 m) long.

Awesome facts
Ceratosaurus had horns on its head, in front of the eyes. These made it look more frightening and may have been used in fighting.

Ceratosaurus

 Q: Why did theropod skulls have so many holes?

A: Holes are lighter than bones, and a light skull can move faster. So flesh-eaters had thin bones with very big holes between them for its ears, eyes, nostrils, and jaw muscles.

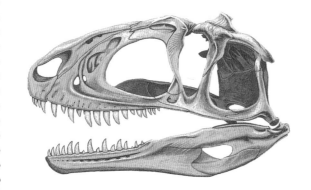

Small and medium-sized flesh-eaters like Ceratosaurus could clearly run fast and they moved at 12-19 mph (20-30 km/h.) That's about the fastest you could sprint over a short distance. Bigger flesh-eaters may not have been able to sprint so fast because they were so much heavier.

Albertosaurus

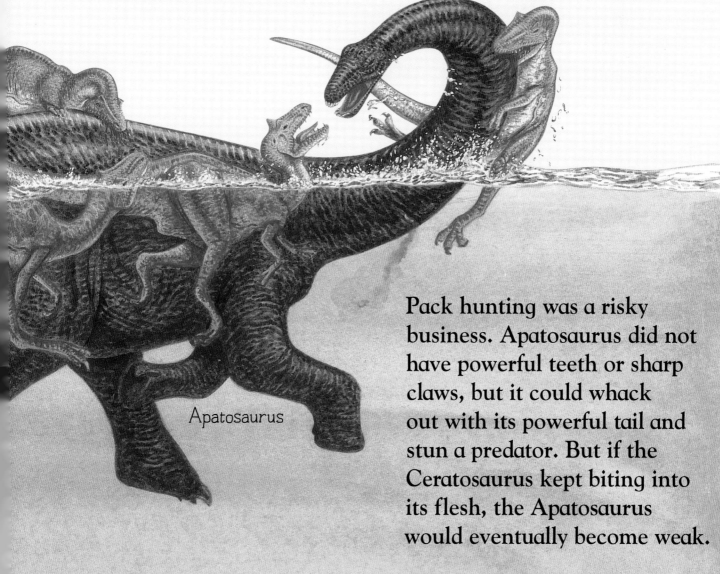

Apatosaurus

Pack hunting was a risky business. Apatosaurus did not have powerful teeth or sharp claws, but it could whack out with its powerful tail and stun a predator. But if the Ceratosaurus kept biting into its flesh, the Apatosaurus would eventually become weak.

WHAT'S IN A NAME?

The first dinosaurs were named nearly 200 years ago. Their names sometimes tell us something about the dinosaur itself. For example, Ceratosaurus, named in 1884, means "horned reptile," referring to the horns on its face.

Q: Who gave dinosaurs their names?

A: Dinosaurs are named by their discoverers. About 10 or 20 new species are still being named every year. If you find a new dinosaur skeleton that has never been named, you can make up a name and publish it!

Richard Owen made up the word "dinosaur" in 1842. It is Greek for "terrible lizard."

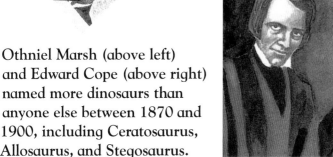

Othniel Marsh (above left) and Edward Cope (above right) named more dinosaurs than anyone else between 1870 and 1900, including Ceratosaurus, Allosaurus, and Stegosaurus.

Megalosaurus, named in 1824, means "big reptile." This drawing shows what scientists then thought it looked like.

Heterodontosaurus

Ceratosaurus

ALL OVER THE WORLD

Meat eaters lived all over the world. Allosaurus, for example, is best known from the Late Jurassic of North America, 150 million years ago, but remains have also been found in Tanzania in Africa, and possibly even in Australia.

The worldwide spread of Allosaurus is not surprising when you remember that the continents were joined together as the supercontinent Pangaea in the Jurassic (see page 5). Allosaurus could have wandered from one end of the world to the other.

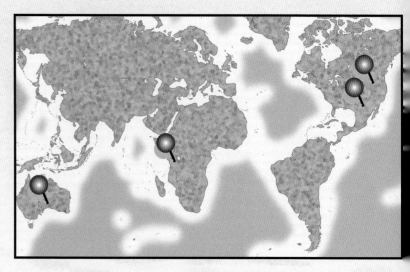

Sites of most Allosaurus finds

Awesome facts
The Australian Allosaurus find is not confirmed. It is in Early Cretaceous rocks, 50 million years younger than the other finds, and is only of part of a leg.

A dinosaur could wander from America to Africa and Australia. Or could it?

zoom in on...

Skull horns

Allosaurus, like most meat eaters, had knobs and lumps on its skull. What were they for? Maybe they just made its face look more scary. When male dinosaurs squared up to each other, the Allosaurus, with its loud growl and big bumps, would usually have been the winner.

Allosaurus

TINY AND TERRIBLE

Some flesh-eaters were so tiny that a big plant-eating dinosaur like Apatosaurus would not even see them. But these midgets were pretty scary if you were a lizard or a rat-like mammal. Small size went with intelligence and speed.

Compsognathus lived in what is now Germany, and was the smallest dinosaur—a mere 2 feet (60 cm) long from its snout to the tip of its tail. One of the amazing fossils of this tiny hunter (right) even shows its last meal—a complete skeleton of the lizard Bavarisaurus inside its rib cage.

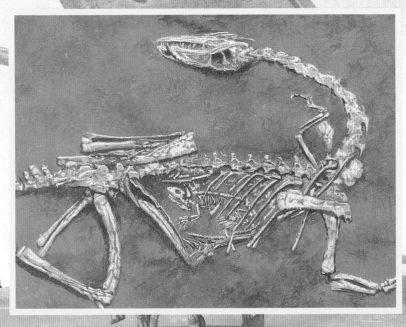

Awesome facts
When Compsognathus was found in 1861, it was not recognized as a dinosaur because it was thought to be too small.

A small flock of Compsognathus are scattered (right) by a giant plant-eater. These little dinosaur could move fast. They may even have had a fine covering of feathers over their bodies. They fed on lizards, frogs, and dragonflies.

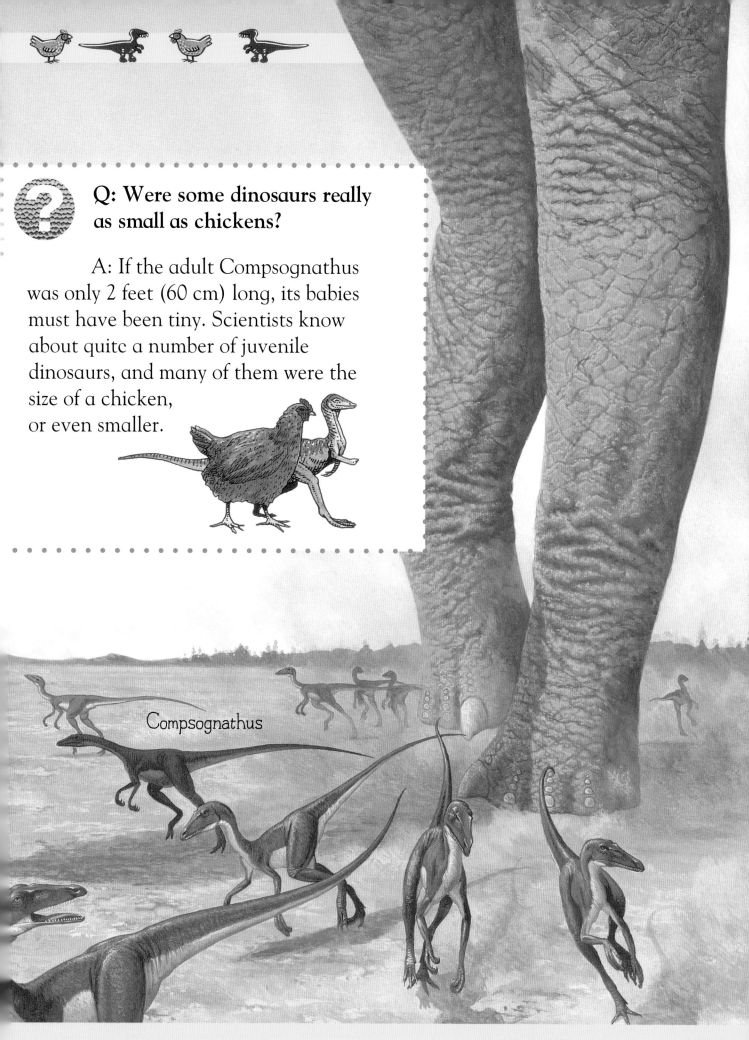

Q: Were some dinosaurs really as small as chickens?

A: If the adult Compsognathus was only 2 feet (60 cm) long, its babies must have been tiny. Scientists know about quite a number of juvenile dinosaurs, and many of them were the size of a chicken, or even smaller.

Compsognathus

FEATHERED FIND

Until the 1990s, feathers on dinosaurs was only a wild theory. Then some startling finds in China proved that many small theropods had them. Sinosauropteryx and Caudipteryx are two of the new Chinese feathered dinosaurs, relatives of Compsognathus. Feathers on dinosaurs proves that birds are living dinosaurs.

Archaeopteryx and Compsognathus were found in the same rocks in southern Germany. They were both named in 1861. Paleontologists soon noticed that the two skeletons were very similar and they suggested that dinosaurs had given rise to birds. This has been debated hotly for years, but it now seems clear that birds really are living theropod dinosaurs.

Archaeopteryx

Feathers are made from keratin, the same protein that makes up your nails and hair. Feathers are not often preserved as fossils because they typically rot away before the carcass is buried. In some cases, if the feather is buried quickly, it will survive as a fossil.

zoom in on...

Wings

A wing is just a fairly long arm that carries feathers. Deinonychus had long arms with strong hands, covered with short feathers. It is not hard to see how this could have evolved into a flying wing if the feathers grew longer.

Deinonychus

FISHING CLAWS

Most theropods ate other dinosaurs or smaller land animals. One group, the spinosaurids, had crocodile-shaped skulls and may have been fish-eaters. Perhaps they used their strong hands to swipe fish out of the water, just as bears do today.

Awesome facts

The spinosaurid Baryonyx from southern England was found by accident in 1983 by William Walker as he walked through his local brick works.

Baryonyx

Q: Why did spinosaurids have crocodile skulls?

A: The long, low snout and numerous teeth of the spinosaurids must have been ideal for holding struggling fish. Stronger jaws are needed only for larger prey. Spinosaurids looked far more like modern crocodiles than other theropods.

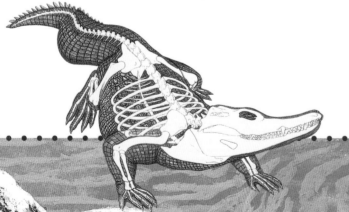

Spinosaurids had long spines on their vertebrae (backbone). These may have carried a thin covering of skin—a kind of sail, running along the backbone. Perhaps the sail was used in controlling body temperature—to take in heat when they were cold and to give off heat when they were overheated.

The spinosaurid Baryonyx, from the Early Cretaceous of southern England, crouches silently beside a river and swipes out a fish with its long-clawed hand.

NESTING

An astonishing find in 1995 in Mongolia showed that some meat eaters sat on their eggs, just like modern birds, to protect them and keep them warm (or cool). Most modern reptiles lay their eggs then leave them.

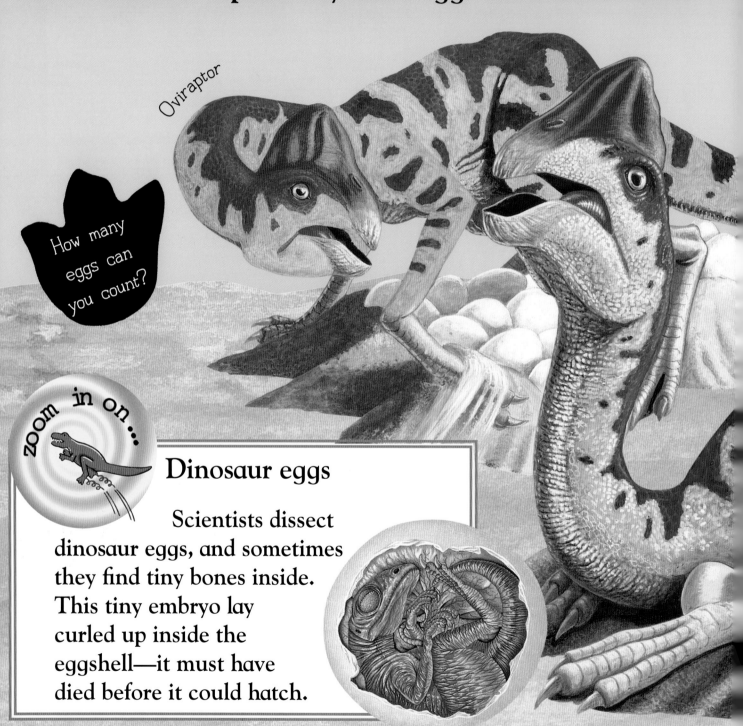

Oviraptor

How many eggs can you count?

zoom in on...

Dinosaur eggs

Scientists dissect dinosaur eggs, and sometimes they find tiny bones inside. This tiny embryo lay curled up inside the eggshell—it must have died before it could hatch.

Oviraptor means "egg thief." It was named in 1924, and has had a bad reputation ever since. Paleontologists then thought this toothless theropod fed on eggs. But the reason it was found close to nests containing eggs was that it was a good parent, caring for its own young!

As good parents, dinosaurs probably helped to protect their young after they had hatched. They may have brought back food, partly chewed, to feed to their young. Disgusting maybe, but that's what many birds do.

SIZING UP

The flesh-eating dinosaur Tyrannosaurus rex, from the Upper Cretaceous of North America, was a monster. At 39 feet (12 m) long and weighing up to 7.5 tons (6.8 t), T. rex was truly awesome: it could swallow you in one gulp. But was it the biggest?

 Q: How big was a T. rex tooth?

A: T. rex had teeth the size of steak knives. The tooth had two halves. The upper crown, which did the cutting business, was the size of a banana. The root, hidden in the jawbone, was just as big.

T. rex—terrifying hunter or humble scavenger? Some paleontologists think that T. rex was so massive that it could not have moved fast. It might have trundled about slowly, looking for rotting carcasses that had been killed by smaller, swifter theropods.

Other huge dinosaurs, such as Carcharodontosaurus from North Africa, and Giganotosaurus from Argentina, may have been longer than T. rex, but they were not as heavy.

zoom in on...

Pooh!

In 2003, Canadian scientists found a giant dinosaur dropping, about 25 inches (64 cm) long, containing dinosaur bones. Whodunnit? T. rex, most probably.

FLESH-EATERS' WORLD

From the tiny Compsognathus to the awesome T. rex, theropods were the terrors of the Mesozoic Era. They are known from all corners of the Earth and existed for 165 million years.

Allosaurus

Can you remember which of these theropods ate fish?

Megalasaurus

250 mya (million years ago)

TRIASSIC

205 mya

JURASSIC

Herrerasaurus

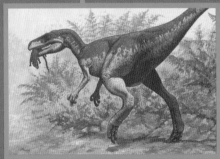

Which of the theropods on these pages lived millions of years before the rest?

Ceratosaurus

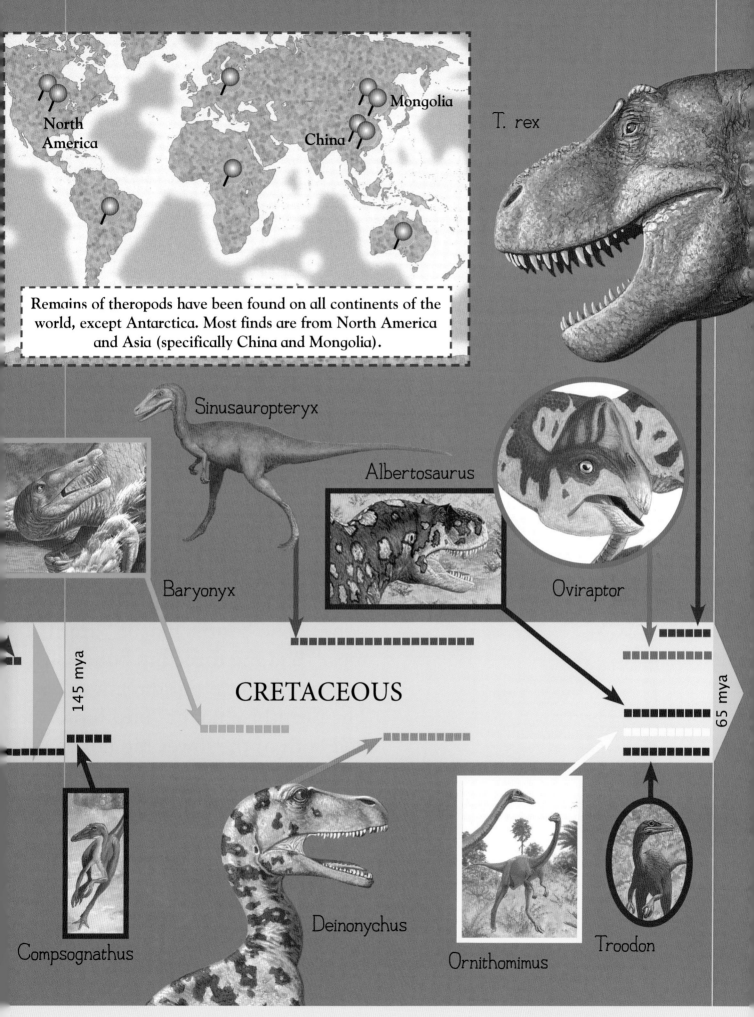

Remains of theropods have been found on all continents of the world, except Antarctica. Most finds are from North America and Asia (specifically China and Mongolia).

North America

Mongolia

China

T. rex

Sinusauropteryx

Albertosaurus

Oviraptor

Baryonyx

145 mya

CRETACEOUS

65 mya

Compsognathus

Deinonychus

Ornithomimus

Troodon

DINOSAUR GROUPS

There were five main groups
of dinosaurs:
two-legged plant eaters
(such as duckbills) called
"ornithopods;" bonehead
and horned dinosaurs, called
"marginocephalians;" armored plant
eaters, called "thyreophorans;" meat eaters,
called "theropods;" and big, long-necked plant
eaters, called "sauropodomorphs."

Tyrannosaurus rex

SAURISCHIA

THEROPODA

SAUROPODOMORPHA

THYREOPHORA

ORNITHISCHIA

MARGINOCEPHALIA

ORNITHOPODA

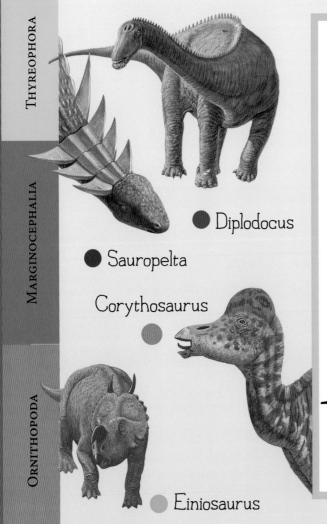

● Diplodocus

● Sauropelta

Corythosaurus

● Einiosaurus

All dinosaurs are classed into one
of two sub-groups—the Saurischia
and the Ornithischia—according to
the arrangement of their three hip
bones. The Saurischia, or "lizard
hips," had the three hip bones all
pointing in different directions.
The Ornithischia, or "bird hips,"
had both of the lower hip bones
running backwards.

Hypsilophodon
(Ornithischia)

Carnotaurus
(Saurischia)

GLOSSARY

Cold-blooded
A cold-blooded animal needs to take its body heat from outside sources like the Sun.

Continental drift
The movement of the continents over time.

Cretaceous
The geological period that lasted from 145 to 65 million years ago.

Cynodont
A mammal-like reptile similar to the very first mammals.

Fossil
The remains of any ancient plant or animal, usually preserved in rock.

Geological
To do with the study of rocks.

Jurassic
The geological period that lasted from 205 to 145 million years ago.

Mammal
A backboned animal with hair that feeds its young on milk, like a cat or a human.

Mesozoic
The "age of dinosaurs"—the geological era that lasted from 250 to 65 million years ago.

Paleontologist
A person who studies fossils.

Pangaea
An ancient supercontinent that consisted of all the modern continents joined together as one.

Predator
A flesh-eater—an animal that hunts others for food.

Radioactive
Describes an element that gives off sub-atomic particles at a fixed rate. Measuring radioactive elements in ancient rocks allows geologists to calculate the age of the rocks.

Radioactivity
The process by which an element gives up sub-atomic particles at a fixed rate.

Reptile
A backboned animal with scales that lives on land and lays eggs, such as a dinosaur, a crocodile, or a lizard.

Scavenger
A flesh-eater that feeds off animals that have died or have been killed by others.

Species
One particular kind of plant or animal, such as Tyrannosaurus rex, the panda, or human beings.

Theropod
A flesh-eating dinosaur.

Triassic
The geological period that lasted from 250 to 205 mya.

Vertebra
(plural Vertebrae)
Together, the vertebrae make up the backbone. Each vertebra is like a cotton reel with bits sticking out for the ribs and muscles.

Warm-blooded
A warm-blooded animal, such as a mammal or a bird, creates heat inside its body from the food it eats.

INDEX

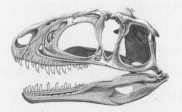